A NEW LIFE

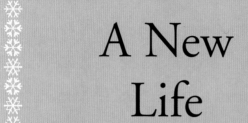

A New
Life

Rukhsana Khan

PICTURES BY

Nasrin Khosravi

GROUNDWOOD BOOKS
HOUSE OF ANANSI PRESS
TORONTO

Groundwood Books / House of Anansi Press
110 Spadina Avenue, Suite 801, Toronto, Ontario M5V 2K4

We acknowledge for their financial support of our publishing program the
Canada Council for the Arts, the Government of Canada through the
Book Publishing Industry Development Program (BPIDP) and the
Ontario Arts Council.

 ONTARIO ARTS COUNCIL
CONSEIL DES ARTS DE L'ONTARIO

Library and Archives Canada Cataloguing in Publication
Khan, Rukhsana
[Coming to Canada]
A new life / Rukhsana Khan; illustrated by Nasrin Khosravi.
Previously published under title: Coming to Canada.
ISBN 978-0-88899-930-6
1. Immigrant children–Canada–Juvenile fiction.
2. Immigrants–Canada–Juvenile fiction. I. Khosravi, Nasrin II. Title.
PS8571.H42C65 2009   jC813'.54   C2008-904887-3

Design by Michael Solomon
Printed and bound in China

With thanks to my parents,
Muhammad Anwar Khan
and Iftikhar Shahzadi Khan,
for bringing me to Canada. — RK

In memory of my late husband,
my biggest inspiration and my best friend,
whom I'll always love and always miss. — NK

CHAPTER ONE

Saying Goodbye

A NEW LAND. A new country. A new home. How exciting!

But Hamza doesn't think so.

"Why do we have to go?" says Hamza.

My father puts down his suitcase and touches Hamza's cheek. "For the schools, the opportunities. I'm doing this for you. Now give me a hug."

Hamza turns away, but Abugee pulls him into his arms and squeezes him tight. When he lets go I can see that Hamza is smiling in spite of himself. Then it's my turn. My father's big arms circle me like a thick blanket and he kisses the top of my head. "You be good for your mother, Khadija. Insha Allah, I'll see you soon. In Canada!"

He sounds excited.

My mother has tears in her eyes. Abugee nods at

her and Amigee nods back, pulling her chador close.

Abugee has to bend down to kiss my grand-mother. Daddiami rubs the top of his head. And then he's gone, to set up a house for us in Canada.

Hamza runs up the stairs and slams the door to his room. A look passes between my mother and grandmother, and then Daddiami follows after him. She walks up the stairs slowly. I could pass her if I wanted to, but I hang back.

Hamza's lying face down on the bed. Is he crying?

Daddiami says, "For shame, Hamza. Stop carrying on. Look at Khadija. How brave she is!"

I grin up at her but Daddiami doesn't notice. She goes onto the veranda. What's she doing out there? I can hear some pots being moved around. Hamza is curious too, and we peek at her from the doorway.

"Come see this."

She's fussing with the jasmine bush. "This plant is too crowded," she says. "There's no room for the young shoots to grow."

She pulls out a little stem that was hiding beneath some of the leaves and pushes it into its own pot of black earth. She pats the soil around it so it's good and firm, then picks up the can of water to give it a drink.

"When a plant is young, it is easy to move," Daddiami says. "It takes time, but eventually it gets used to its new place. New roots will grow and new leaves will sprout. It's difficult to move a mature plant and you cannot move a plant that is old. You'll only kill it. It will miss the soil it grew up in and die of homesickness.

"It will be hard for your parents, even harder than it will be for you. You must be strong. And you must make it easy for them. I'm counting on you."

CHAPTER TWO

The Arrival

THIS NEW COUNTRY of Canada is cold, but at least it's raining. I've always liked the rain. It doesn't rain much in Pakistan.

Hamza's in a foul mood. He misses Daddiami. So do I, but that doesn't mean I can't be excited too.

There is so much to look at as we wait in line with our passports. The people are so tall and so white. And they're dressed so stylishly, their hair clipped neatly.

The lady officer we report to is wearing lots of make-up and she has fluffy yellow hair. I wish I could touch it. I wonder what it feels like.

I don't like the way she looks at Amigee. It makes me see her in a different way. I never noticed how shabby Amigee looks. But that's from the

flight, isn't it? Hamza said we sat for sixteen hours. All the passengers look shabby, don't they?

The fancy doors open sideways when we get close to them. I barely have time to wonder how they knew we were coming, because I see Abugee pressed against the barrier on the other side.

He looks older. I'm sure there is more grey hair at the sides of his face. But when he wraps me in his big arms, it feels exactly the same.

I can't wait to see our new home. I've seen pictures of houses in North America on TV. They're always clean and stylish.

But the house that Abugee has set up for us isn't even a house. It's an apartment, just a few rooms. And the furniture is used and has scratches and dents.

Abugee looks sorry. "One day we'll have money to buy whatever we want," he promises Amigee.

Hamza wrinkles up his nose at it, but I think my bed is real bouncy.

•

THE VERY NEXT DAY Amigee takes us to the school to register. She struggles to speak English, but the lady at the desk goes over to an office that has a sign on the door and calls, "Mrs. Shankar!"

That sounds Indian and Mrs. Shankar is Indian, but when she comes towards us she looks strange and uncomfortable. She's wearing the same kind of clothes as the lady at the desk, but they're rumpled and too tight.

Hamza nudges me. "Doesn't she look silly? She thinks she's white!" Amigee squeezes his arm and he is quiet.

Mrs. Shankar's accent is strange but at least we can understand her. "Have you brought your documents? We need your landed immigrant papers, immunization records and birth certificates. And do you have health card numbers and a copy of a bill to prove that you live in the area?"

We don't have most of those papers, so Amigee has to call Abugee and he uses his taxi to take us around to get them. First we go to get our health cards, then this place, then that place with lots of standing in line. The next day we visit the doctor's office where we get some needles. Ow!

A few days later we're finally set. We've got every piece of paper we need.

On our first day of school I get up extra early. I clean my teeth and brush my hair and put on some socks. They feel funny on my feet, but Abugee says we have to get used to wearing them. I gulp down my breakfast. Hamza's still in the bathroom taking a shower but I've already got my coat and boots on and I'm waiting at the door.

The nice thing about Canada is that there's always water in the taps. Not like Pakistan where it only flowed for about an hour, twice a day. And there's warm water! You can take a shower or bath any time you want because you don't have to wait to warm up the water on the stove. Hamza takes a shower every day now, but I still only want one twice a week.

Amigee riffles through the papers making sure we have everything and then we walk to school. By the time Mrs. Shankar has helped us fill out all the forms, classes have already started. Amigee bends down to hug and kiss us. "Be good," she says, mostly to Hamza.

Hamza doesn't answer. He just looks down at the floor. Amigee pushes his chin up with her knuckle and looks right into his eyes. "You be good."

Hamza nods and Amigee stands up straight and walks to the big front door. She looks back at us only once and then leaves.

The principal walks us down the hall. It's so empty. It feels like we're the only ones in the school. Her high heels echo on the clean bare floor. The school looks old and shabby. I thought it would be sparkling new, but I guess this is an older part of town.

We go to Hamza's class first because it's closer. They put him in grade five.

The principal knocks and there are fluttery feelings in my stomach. Did Hamza just gulp? He must be nervous too.

The door opens and the principal walks into a bright room. The windows are huge, stretching up almost to the ceiling, and at first the light is all I can see.

And then I see all the faces staring at us. About thirty grade five students. Mostly they're white, but I see a few dark faces among them. The teacher has a broad face and narrow eyes. Is he Chinese? The principal is talking to him and the students. I think she's introducing us, but it sounds like this: "Gudmor ning clas deezar nu stoodens HAMZA und KHADIJA. I hope yool maycdem walcum."

Hamza whispers, "They look like they want to eat me."

"Ssh," I say. "A few of them are smiling."

At least I think they're smiling. The principal takes me away to my class and the last thing I see as the door closes is Hamza's worried face.

Now it's my turn. My hands are sweaty.

When we get to my classroom the principal smiles and says, "Dis iz yonu clas room. I hope yoolbee hapee heer."

She's waiting for me to say something, so I just nod and then she opens the door.

Phew! There must be a big difference between these grade three kids and grade five kids, because the faces look pretty friendly.

I hear the principal say my name and all the kids look at me. Then she says, "I wan evree wun toobee nis tooer." And she says some other stuff too, and then she leaves.

The teacher, Ms. Thomson, hands me a textbook and takes me to sit beside a pretty girl with a pink ribbon in her hair. By the way the girl points and nudges me I figure out I'm supposed to open my textbook.

I look at the pictures while Ms. Thomson starts her lesson.

•

ABUGEE LIKED taking us places when we lived in Pakistan. We drove all over the country. He liked the old places best. He would teach us history as we looked at the beautiful buildings the Moghuls had built. The first time he took us to the Shalimar Gardens it was a hot sunny day and people were splashing in the pools to cool off.

I was little then and I begged so hard that Amigee finally let me go into one of the pools with Hamza. I had to tiptoe to touch the bottom. I kept my neck stretched up just so I could breathe. When people splashed I got a mouthful of water and started to cough. It was scary but I didn't want Amigee

to take me out, so I pretended everything was fine.

That feeling of not being able to swim and hardly being able to touch the bottom is kind of how I feel as I try to learn English. I can hardly understand what people are saying. In Ms. Thomson's class, they talk so fast. Every once in a while they say a word I know. But by the time I realize it, they've moved on to say something else.

In the afternoon I am pulled out of the class with two other girls. One girl is about my colour and the other is much darker. We go to a special teacher named Mrs. Baker to learn to speak English. From the first moment, I love Mrs. Baker. She's so gentle. She talks nice and slow, and she always gives me a chance to think of how to answer. There are eight other kids in our class.

We point at ourselves and say our names. The two girls from my class are Margarita and Rada. Margarita is the one who's my colour and she's from Nicaragua. Rada is from Somalia.

I've never seen hair like Rada's. It's fuzzy, like wool. I want to touch it, but I've learned it's not polite.

On the way home I see Margarita and Rada walking ahead. They turn right into the walkway of our own building. It turns out that Margarita lives on the fifth floor and Rada's on the eleventh.

That night at supper I tell my parents about my new friends.

Abugee takes out his atlas and we look for Nicaragua and Somalia, and then we find Pakistan. They're so far apart. With our fingers we trace a line across the oceans, across the different-coloured countries, all the way here to Canada. It's a long way.

Abugee says there are many people from all over the world in this country. How do they all get along?

CHAPTER THREE

School Days

A WEEK HAS passed and I'm starting to get used to the school schedule, but I still jump when the recess bell rings. It sounds so shrill and loud. The other kids don't even flinch. In fact they look happy, so I try to pretend I'm not nervous.

First the teacher makes us line up at a white boxy thing that sticks out of the wall. It has a knob on the side that you turn and a little shiny part at the top where water squirts out. All the other kids are eager to stick their tongues in the water, and they linger so the teacher has to count their turn – 1, 2, 3… I try to look eager too, but what good is wetting your tongue? I wish I had a cup. I could angle it towards that stream of water and fill it up. I'd just love a drink of water!

When we get out into the yard the kids are running and screaming, bouncing balls and skipping rope.

Where's Hamza? There are so many children, it's hard to see him. He's not by the sandbox, not by the grassy field.

There he is by the corner of the school building. He's got his hands shoved in his pockets and a scowl on his face.

He says, "These people with their fancy clothes and their expensive shoes and the way they look

down their noses at you because you don't have those things yet."

"Not everyone's like that. Some of them have been nice to me."

"That's because you're only in grade three. Wait till you get to my age. Then you'll see the way they really are."

A big girl runs by to catch a ball but she stops when she sees us. "Hamza!"

She calls over her shoulder to the others. They talk a bit, then one of them nods. "C'mon," she says.

I take a step forward and she glances at me but doesn't tell me "no," so I guess I can go too.

They're playing a weird kind of cricket. But their bat isn't flat, it's round like a broomstick. And there's no wicket. And they don't bowl the ball. They throw it over a flat thing on the ground. Hamza's playing in the field. I get to chase down the stray balls.

When the bell rings I wait for Hamza to catch up. "See? They're being nice to you. They let you play."

"I didn't get to bat."

"Maybe your team didn't have a turn yet."

"Didn't you see them change? The other team told me to stay out in the field too."

"Maybe they thought you'd rather field."

Hamza gives me a look like I've said something really silly.

•

THE NEXT DAY I spend recess trying to cheer up Hamza again. When the same girl calls him to play that game that's like cricket but isn't cricket, Hamza points at the bat and makes a move to show he wants to swing it.

The girl frowns and points to the outfield. Hamza crosses his arms and leans against the side of the school.

"See?" Hamza says. "They're never going to let

me bat. Did you see the way those guys looked at me?"

I nod. It wasn't very nice. Maybe Hamza is right.

He says, "They think we're poor, just because we don't have fancy stuff like they have. They think we're not as good as they are."

"But we're not poor," I say. "We had nice things in Pakistan. Don't they know we can't afford them right now? Abugee's saving as much as he can. It's just going to take time, like Daddiami said."

"I'm tired of waiting."

Margarita and Rada come towards me. They have a skipping rope. An immigrant-looking rope. It isn't as nice as the other girls' ropes. It must have broken because there's a big fat knot in the middle. Maybe it'll be hard to jump over that knot, but I'd still like to try.

I look over at Hamza. Will he mind?

Hamza's scowling again. "Why don't you just go with your *friends*. Leave me alone."

Does he mean it? But then I see his bottom lip quivering. I look away before Hamza sees that I'm staring. In Pakistan, he was the one with lots of friends.

Rada nudges me with the skipping rope. I shake my head and step closer to Hamza. Rada turns and goes off with Margarita. I wish I could go with them.

For a while Hamza and I watch the other kids play, but it gets really boring. We can't just stand here all recess. So I ask, "Do you have Mrs. Baker for English too?"

"What do you think?"

"I'm just asking!"

"What a stupid question. Who else would I have? All the kids who can't speak English have to go to her."

We're quiet for a few moments. Hamza glares at the kids playing that game then he says, "I bet they don't know I can read. And I even know a few words in English. I bet they think I'm stupid. I'd like to show them!"

"Stop it!"

Hamza looks surprised.

"Just stop it." And for once he does. For the rest

of recess we stand there watching all the other kids play. He doesn't say one word, but his temper is boiling up inside. I can tell.

The bell rings and we march back into the school. One of the kids in Hamza's class is right beside him. He looks mean, and he says something but I can't hear it.

Then Hamza stops by a little red box that's stuck on the wall. That kid from his class says something to him again. There are words written on the little red box in white letters. Hamza stands in front of it with all the other kids jostling past him and reads "P-U-L-L." Pull. So he does.

Immediately a different bell starts ringing. It's very loud and urgent, and the teachers look scared. The mean kid laughs. The teachers yell something and tell everyone to go back outside. We line up in rows according to our classes.

The principal comes storming out, talking to the teachers. Then that mean kid in Hamza's class, the one who told him to do it, points right at him. The tattletale.

In front of the whole school Hamza's teacher Mr. Oyoung pulls him forward to face the princi-

pal. They call Mrs. Shankar to join them too. Are they going to beat Hamza? His face is red. He's standing so still, like he's turned into a statue.

Mrs. Shankar speaks to the principal quietly. Her eyes grow wide and she stares at Hamza.

I can't stand it any longer. I run towards Mrs. Shankar yelling, "It was an accident. He didn't know!"

Mrs. Shankar tells me to go back to my place in line. Rada puts an arm around me, and I feel a little better.

Then Mrs. Shankar bends close to Hamza and says, "You pulled the fire alarm. It's against the rules. You can't do that. You mustn't ever do that again. Okay?"

Hamza's face is so serious. He nods and then he says quietly, "Are you going to tell my parents?"

Mrs. Shankar frowns. "No. I don't think that's necessary. Just don't ever do that again. Not unless there's a fire. Okay?"

Hamza nods. And one by one the teachers file their classes back into the school.

That's it? No beating? They didn't even yell at him. But maybe they're saving it for when he gets back to the classroom.

All afternoon in Mrs. Baker's class I try not to worry, but it's hard.

I can't wait to see if Hamza's all right. When he comes out of his class he looks fine. I don't see any bruises and he's not crying.

I can't ask Hamza while we're walking home with Amigee. And I can't ask him at dinnertime. It's not until we're tucked into our beds that I can ask him what happened.

"Nothing," he says. "What you saw. That was it."

"But what about the other kids? Didn't they make fun of you?"

"Nope. That's the strangest thing. They started being nice to me. Really nice."

"But you're not going to pull the alarm again, are you?"

"Of course not! I wouldn't have done it the first time if I'd known what it was."

The very next day that same girl asks Hamza to play again, and this time they let him swing the bat. Hamza swings three times without hitting the ball, and they tell him he's "out" and has to give the next

person a turn. When the teams change, he goes back to playing outfield, but this time he doesn't seem to mind. He even looks a bit happier.

•

ABOUT A WEEK later, we arrive home after a long day of school. We haven't even taken our coats off when Amigee says, "What have you done?" She's staring at Hamza. Did she find out about the fire alarm?

Hamza's face turns red and he looks at the floor.

"Tell me right now and you won't get into so much trouble with your father."

I hold my breath, waiting for Hamza to tell, but instead he shrugs. "I didn't do anything."

Amigee looks doubtful. Hamza looks straight up at her without blinking. For a few moments they just stand there, frozen. And then, finally, Amigee turns away. "Never mind," she says. "We'll find out soon enough. Your teacher called and we have to meet him tonight."

Amigee calls Mrs. Korczak from next door to look after us. And then she goes into the kitchen to begin supper. We can finally take off our coats.

Hamza looks worried. I nudge him and say, "Do you think it's about the fire alarm?"

"I don't think so. They said they wouldn't tell, and even if they were going to, they wouldn't have waited this long."

When Abugee hears the news his face gets dark and he stares at Hamza. "What did you do?"

"Nothing."

"Then why would they call? You must have done something."

"No. I've been good."

"Are you lying?"

"No, Abugee. Honest."

"We'll see about that."

Mrs. Korczak comes over after supper. She takes off her shawl and hangs it on the hook. Then she plops down in front of the TV.

"We won't be long," calls Amigee.

Mrs. Korczak cups her hand around her ear. "Eh?"

"WE WON'T BE LONG!"

Mrs. Korczak nods and turns back to the TV.

When the door closes behind them, Hamza says, "Let's go to bed before they get back. They can't yell at me if I'm asleep. They'll have to wait till tomorrow, and by then they won't be so angry. If it is anything."

"But *did* you do something?" I ask.

Hamza scowls. "NO!"

"Okay, okay. I was just wondering."

We get all ready for bed. Hamza sits near the window, glancing down at the street for any sign of our parents. In the middle of a really funny show, he cries, "They're coming."

We rush into the bedroom. Lights out, try to get to bed. Ow! I bumped my shin!

"Sssh!" says Hamza.

I pull up the covers just as the key turns in the lock. They're talking quietly. Amigee is saying what a nice walk it was. Abugee is agreeing with her. Then Amigee says, "THANK YOU VERY MUCH,

Mrs. Korczak!" And pretty soon the door closes behind her. Now will they start yelling?

Abugee says, "Hamza?"

"Ssh. They're sleeping," Amigee says. "And look, they didn't forget to do their chores."

The light from the hallway casts their shadows across my blankets and against the wall.

Amigee says, "They really are very good, don't you think?"

"His teacher said so. How can we argue?"

Amigee says, "We'll show him the extra work Mr. Oyoung wants him to do tomorrow."

Quietly they shut the door.

I whisper, "Hamza? You awake?"

"Yeah."

"Did you hear that?"

"Yeah."

"Doesn't sound like they're mad at all."

"See? Told you I was good."

He rolls over, and in a few moments I can hear him breathing heavily.

CHAPTER FOUR

A Dragon in a Book

Months have gone by. I know quite a bit of English now. So does Hamza. I only spend an hour in Mrs. Baker's class these days, not the whole afternoon. She's teaching me how to read English properly. In Pakistan, we learned the alphabet and how to read a few words, so it's not too hard. Especially now that I know what most of the words mean.

Today Mrs. Baker has a surprise for me. It's a big brown box with some writing on the side.

"Open it," she says.

"What's inside?"

"You'll see."

I struggle with the tape till she hands me a pair of scissors. I pull out the packing material to find a pile of books. Special books just for me and

Hamza, where the story is written in English and Urdu!

Mrs. Baker already has some books with Somali for Rada, and some with Spanish for Margarita and even some with other languages.

She says, "Why don't you read to us?"

The English words are a bit hard. I struggle to sound them out. Mrs. Baker says, "No, no. Read it in Urdu."

"But you won't understand."

"Okay, I'll read the English and then you read the Urdu."

And so we read together and I do my best. Rada

and Margarita and the other kids all listen carefully. Then Mrs. Baker takes a turn with Margarita reading her English and Spanish book.

Mrs. Baker lets me borrow my book. She wants Amigee to read it to me in Urdu tonight.

A few weeks later, Mrs. Baker takes us to the school library. Today I'm going to pick a chapter book. I find one with a picture of a shiny gold dragon on the cover. I take it to the table and open it to the first page.

I sound out the words like Mrs. Baker showed me: "The dra-gon flew o-ver the moun-tain and …" All of a sudden the words on the page disappear, and I can see a dragon beating its wings!

Am I going crazy? I shake my head and look up. It breaks the spell.

The dragon's gone. I'm back here, in the school library. There's Mrs. Baker helping Margarita choose a book, and there's Rada reading something about a kitten. Okay. Let's try this again.

"The dragon flew over the mountain and saw a witch on the other side."

Again the words vanish and I see a dragon and a witch on a broomstick.

Does this happen to everyone, or is it just me? I read it again and this time I don't stop.

Wow! Reading a book is like making a movie in

my head, and I'm the star. Well, actually, right now I'm a dragon.

I swear it's magical!

•

ABUGEE HAS gotten grumpy. Maybe he's tired. He drives a taxi during the day, and then he has to go to school at night and on weekends. Sometimes I hear him grumble. Some of his customers are mean to him.

He's waiting to get his university degree from Pakistan approved. So many rules and regulations, he says. And he has to go to school to improve his English so he can be a substitute teacher, even though he was a principal back in Pakistan. If he can just get his teacher's certificate, things will be better.

Today Hamza and I make too much noise when he is trying to sleep. He yells at us and then stomps back to bed. I bump Hamza with one of his cars but he shoos me away. He says he is thinking up a plan to make Abugee happy.

When Abugee finally gets up, Hamza says, "Can we go to the library? My teacher says it has all kinds of interesting stuff."

Abugee's eyes light up. It was the perfect thing for Hamza to say. Amigee says she'll come too.

The library isn't very far so we walk. Abugee is happy to be out of his taxi. The library is in a big building. Inside it is very tidy with wall-to-wall carpet and some people at computers and others reading quietly at desks.

Abugee gestures to all the books. "Here you see the real treasure of this country."

Hamza wrinkles his forehead. "Books?"

"Not just books! Knowledge! This is why we came here. This will help us make a better life. This

library contains all the best information you can find. And it's available to everyone in the land, both rich and poor. And it's free."

Abugee takes Hamza to look at the non-fiction section. Hamza wants to know about sharks and dinosaurs and hockey. I go over to the chapter books and get one about a beautiful horse.

Even Amigee chooses a book. It's in Urdu. That's so nice of them to have books that we can read.

By the time we go home, Abugee is in a much better mood.

I show Hamza the book I got. He doesn't look that interested, so I say, "You know what? When I read in English something magical happens!" And I tell him about the movie in my head.

Hamza says, "Don't be silly! It's not magic. It happens when you read Urdu books too." Then he picks up one of the books we brought with us from Pakistan and tells me to start reading.

He's right! The pictures form in the very same way.

"How come I didn't see them before?"

"You have to get good enough at reading first."

He makes it sound so ordinary!

Never mind. I still think it's magical.

•

WHILE I AM waiting to walk home with Hamza, some bully kids call me names and say I am stinky. It makes me cry. When Hamza sees me he knows something is wrong. He makes me tell him about it. He gets so mad. "Show me them," he says.

They are in the sandbox.

Hamza starts marching towards them. I pull at his shirt saying, "Just ignore them."

But he won't. He chases them down and there's a fight.

It's two against one, but Hamza still beats them.

The school calls home and Hamza gets in trouble. Abugee yells at him, telling him he's throwing away his chances. Amigee looks sad. Hamza just sits there and listens. He doesn't tell them it was all because of me.

When they're done and he's promised not to fight again, he comes into our room. "Are you okay?" I say.

He shrugs. He's going to hop into his bed but then he turns and says, "You know you really should take a bath every day. You do kind of smell."

It hurts my feelings when he says that. It bothers me for two whole days. But I decide to listen and now I make myself take a bath every single day.

It makes a big difference.

•

IT'S TRUE THAT our home is much shabbier than in Pakistan, but even here there are those who have it worse. Margarita's apartment is a lot like ours, but it's much smaller. And it smells different. Her mom gave me a burrito with beans and salad inside. It was delicious.

After I bug Rada for a long time, she finally gets permission for me to visit. Rada's house smells different too. She lives in a two-bedroom apartment like ours, but instead of sharing a room with a brother, she doesn't even have a room. Her uncle's family has one bedroom, and her mother and father and baby brother have the other. Rada sleeps with her sister in the living room on a sofa that turns into a bed at night.

"Where's your study area?" I ask.

Rada looks at me like I said something weird.

It's just past four o'clock when a strange man shuffles down the hallway.

"That's my uncle," she whispers. "He doesn't have a job yet so he likes to sit on the sofa and watch TV till really late at night."

"But how can you sleep if he's sitting on your sofa bed?"

Rada shrugs. "We can't. We have to wait till he goes to bed."

No wonder she's so sleepy during the day.

Rada's mother looks very tired. She works as an assistant cook in a senior citizens' home even

though she was a nurse and midwife back in Somalia.

"Let's go find Margarita and we can play ball downstairs," I say.

Rada looks doubtful but she goes to her mother and asks anyway. Her mother glances at me but shakes her head. "You know it's too dangerous."

It's not dangerous!

Rada sighs. "She never lets me out of the apartment except to go to school."

When I tell Amigee what Rada's mom said, I expect her to laugh, but she doesn't.

Amigee says, "She's right. It isn't safe."

Abugee says, "It isn't that bad. There are problems everywhere."

Amigee agrees, and they are both silent for a while. Finally, Abugee says, "Some people have come from places where there was war. Maybe they're just glad to be safe for a while. And maybe they are too scared to let their children out of their sight. It takes time to adjust."

I invite Rada and Margarita to my house but Rada isn't allowed to come. She has to help take care of her baby brother. When Margarita arrives we make our own kind of burritos with some of our rotis and a bit of minced beef cooked in Pakistani spices.

Margarita takes a big bite and says, "Rotis and tortillas are practically the same thing."

I think she's right.

•

IT'S CLOSE to the end of the school year and the days are hot and sticky. Especially today and I'm so thirsty. I'd do anything for a cup so I could get a drink of water. It's recess time and I'm so desperate, I'm even eager to line up and wet my tongue in the water fountain.

It's finally my turn. Somehow I breathe in when the stream of water touches my lips. The water! It goes right into my mouth, just like drinking from a cup!

So that's what this thing is for! They weren't just wetting their tongues. They were actually drinking the water!

Gulp, gulp, gulp!

"1, 2, 3… next!" But I still want more. This time I'm the one they nudge to let the next kid have a turn. But at least I'll never be thirsty at school again!

CHAPTER FIVE

Now for the Rest of Canada

I'M IN GRADE five now and it's my turn to have Mr. Oyoung as a teacher. He's nice but gives us way too much homework. I hardly see Mrs. Baker at all except when I go downstairs after school to visit her.

There are new kids who've come to the school from countries far away. When I see them looking so nervous and scared, it makes me remember how I felt and I try to be nice to them.

One day when we get home from school Abugee is already there. He looks tired and happy at the same time. "It's a wonderful day," he tells us. "I just got my teacher's certificate!"

"Does this mean no more taxi?" Amigee asks.

Abugee shakes his head. "No, the money is

good. But now I can substitute teach as well. It's a way to get my foot in the door."

Abugee worked so hard and he only has his foot in the door? How long will it take before he gets his whole self in?

After that Abugee works twice as hard. He wants to make enough money to buy a house.

Amigee decides to help. She gets a job at a coffee shop. The first day of work she wears her uniform: a pair of pants and a shirt. The clothes are kind of tight, and Amigee looks a bit uncomfortable, just like Mrs. Shankar.

Hamza stares at Amigee but doesn't say one word.

•

WHEN ABUGEE finally gets his first full-time job as a teacher, he quits being a taxi driver. To celebrate, Abugee and Amigee decide to take us on a trip before the next school year begins.

Abugee trades in the taxi for a mini van, the kind where the seats fold underneath and we can sleep on the floor. We're going to drive all the way to the Yukon to see some of this big new country of ours.

We drive up through the forests of Ontario to

the flat grass prairies of Manitoba and Saskatchewan, where breezes ripple through fields like waves on the ocean.

Canada is so vast. It takes us a week just to get to Calgary. Hamza knows the names of some of the towns we pass through because his favourite hockey players come from there.

We first catch a glimpse of the Rocky Mountains in Alberta. Their sharp peaks poke the sky and have snow on them, even in the summertime. Those mountains keep us company all the way up the coast of British Columbia.

In the Yukon there is so much purple fireweed. We see moose and even bears right by the side of the road! And when we shut off the engine, the silence presses against our ears.

We stop at all kinds of museums and shops. On the main road in Whitehorse we meet a Native family: a mother, father and brother and sister, kind of like us. They look at us and we look at them. They smile at us and we smile at them. And then we nod and they nod back, and we go on our way.

The next summer we go down east, to Nova Scotia and New Brunswick, and then up north to Newfoundland. Hamza likes the ferry ride to Newfoundland. We see icebergs in the water and

know it's too cold to swim. The best is when we go whale watching. Hamza is the first to spot a dark grey whale when it comes up to breathe. He cries, "Thar she blows!" just like they do in the movies we've seen. All the other tourists laugh.

Even Hamza has to admit that this country is amazing.

When we get back it feels like our apartment has shrunk, or maybe it's me who has grown.

•

YEARS HAVE passed and things have changed. We got our citizenship papers at a special ceremony with a judge and everything. We really are

Canadian now. We have every right to be here and the exact same rights as any other Canadian.

Hamza joined a junior hockey league. Abugee bought him used equipment. He's a great defense-man.

We have a house now with a veranda that Daddiami would love. We put some plants on it, just like she did in Pakistan.

She's coming to visit, and we're cleaning and painting and making the place look its very best for her arrival. Still, there's something missing.

Amigee drives me to the big department store. "What is it you want, Khadija?" she says.

I shrug. I'll know it when I see it.

Up and down the aisles past wallpaper and ceramic tiles, something pulls me towards the garden section. And then I see it. A little jasmine plant. It's perfect.

A jasmine plant grow-ing in a shop in Canada!

It even has some buds on it. I bet they will open by the time Daddiami comes.

THE END

GLOSSARY

Abugee: father
Amigee: mother
Burrito: tortilla stuffed with meat or beans
Chador: shawl
Daddiami: grandmother (father's mother)
Insha Allah: Arabic phrase meaning "if God wills"
Moghuls: dynasty of Muslim rulers, beginning with
    Babur and ending with Aurangzeb, who ruled India
    from the sixteenth to the beginning of the eighteenth
    centuries. They were most famous for their beautiful
    style of architecture, which includes the Taj Mahal
    and the Shalimar Gardens.
Roti: Indian bread (thin flat bread)
Shalimar Gardens: three terraced gardens in Lahore,
    Pakistan, which date back to the Moghul empire
Tortilla: Hispanic bread (thin flat bread)
Urdu: one of the languages spoken in Pakistan and India